To my lovely trolls who liked to dress up when they were little—Maris, Isa, and especially my dancing Mushroom

First US edition 2023

Library of Congress Catalog Card Number 2022923390
ISBN 978-1-5362-3332-2 (English hardcover)
ISBN 978-1-5362-3333-9 (Spanish hardcover)

WOR 28 27 26 25 24 23
10 9 8 7 6 5 4 3 2 1

Printed in Stevens Point, WI, USA

This book was typeset in Copse.
The illustrations were done in mixed media.

Candlewick Press
99 Dover Street
Somerville, Massachusetts 02144

www.candlewick.com

CANDLEWICK PRESS

VLAD
THE FABULOUS VAMPIRE

BEWARE!
Flying trolls

FLAVIA Z. DRAGO

Deep in the
Dark Woods, in an
ancient shadowy castle,
there once lived a
stylish vampire—

Vladislav Varnaby
Roland Dragul,
the fourth of his name.

For Vlad, fashion was his passion. And like all of his vampire friends, he dressed only in black.

Black was elegant.

Black was fun.

Black was
mysterious—
an all-time
classic!

But lurking beneath his black cape,
Vlad kept a colorful secret . . .

Vlad had rosy pink cheeks!
They made him look
different from everyone
else—so horribly alive!

That's why Vlad was always
hiding his pinkness behind
the same old boring outfit
over and over again.

He just wanted to look and feel . . .

like any other paranormal vampire!

One night, Vlad tried to talk about his secret with his best friend . . .

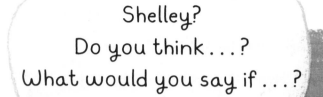

But he just couldn't find the words.

He worried his friends
would stop liking him if they
discovered who he really was.

And then inspiration struck.

Vlad was going to design
his very own clothes!

He worked his fingers
to the bone,

and finally . . .

he found a new way to cover
his face while also looking
fabulous in black!

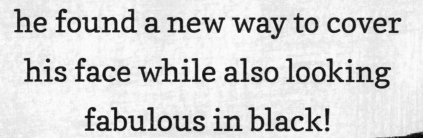

VAMP

After all, fashion
was his passion.

But sooner rather than later, Vlad had a new realization.

Even with the most splendid black garments

and sophisticated style,

he would never be able to hide
who he truly was.

No one understands how I feel, he thought.

WARNING!
FLYING TROLLS

And so Vlad decided
that he'd be better
off alone.

As Vlad left
his friends behind,
he heard something strange.

Shelley was in trouble!

Keep your paws
off my bat hat, troll!

And guess what . . .

She had a secret of her own!

Are you OK?

Please don't tell anyone!

Finally, Vlad decided to share what
he hadn't been able to before.

Do you still like me?

Of course I do!

And in return, Shelley decided
to show him something else . . .

something
no other vampire had
ever seen before!

Together, they went
beyond the borders of the
Dark Woods . . .

and adventured
into the unknown.

With Shelley by his side,
Vlad felt a new kind
of confidence.

Slowly, he began to understand that in order to feel good about himself,

he didn't have to change,

and he didn't need to hide.

Instead, he began to think,

It's better to love what makes us unique!

FANGS

Back home, and with Shelley's help, Vlad was ready to show everyone his true self.

It took a lot of courage.
But as we know, fashion
was his passion!

Of course, there were lots of times
when Vlad still felt insecure.

But when he did, there was always
someone he could count on.

He felt safe, loved, and free!

And in the end, whether you can see it or not . . .

you might just say
that there is a little bit
of Vlad in all of us.

LA CATRINA